DOWNERS GROVE PUBLIC LIBRARY

3 119

W9-BFO-677

AN 2 9 2004

WITHDRAWN
DOWNERS GROVE PUBLIC LIBRARY

IN F WAI
Waid, Mark.
Ruse

Downers Grove Public Library
1050 Curtiss St.
Downers Grove, IL 60515

ENTER THE DETECTIVE

Publisher's Cataloging in Publication Data

Ruse. Volume one : enter the detective / Writer: Mark Waid ; Penciler: Butch Guice ; Inker: Mike Perkins ; Colorist: Laura DePuy.

p. : ill. ; cm.

Spine title: Ruse. 1 : enter the detective

ISBN: 1-931484-19-8

1. Mystery fiction. 2. Graphic novels. 3. Archard, Simon (Fictitious character) 4. Bishop, Emma (Fictitious character) I. Waid, Mark. II. Guice, Butch. III. Perkins, Mike. IV. DePuy, Laura. V. Title: Enter the detective VI. Title: Ruse. 1 : enter the detective.

PN6728 .R87 2002
813.54 [Fic]

RUSE ™
ENTER THE DETECTIVE

Mark **WAID**
W R I T E R

Butch **GUICE**
P E N C I L E R

Mike **PERKINS**
I N K E R

Laura **DePUY**
C O L O R I S T

CHAPTER 6

Jeff **JOHNSON** · PENCILER
Paul **NEARY** · INKER
Jason **LAMBERT** · COLORIST

Dave **LANPHEAR** · LETTERER

COVER ART BY: Butch Guice & Laura DePuy

CrossGeneration Comics   Oldsmar, Florida

ENTER THE DETECTIVE

features Chapters One through Six
from the ongoing series RUSE.

BARONESS BEGUILING

❧ OUR PLAYERS ❧

SIMON ARCHARD
THE CITY'S FAVORITE SON, HIS MIND IS RAZOR-SHARP

EMMA BISHOP
A FETCHING BEAUTY, HER SPIRIT CRAVES ADVENTURE

MIRANDA CROSS
A MYSTERIOUS VISITOR, SOMETHING BUBBLES BENEATH HER SURFACE

SHE VISITS OUR SHORES

PARTINGTON societal circles are awhirl with the arrival of one Miranda Cross, Baroness of the Eastern land of Kharibast. According to her local hosts, Lord and Lady Wainscott of the Blumjuine district, Baroness Cross plans to set up permanent residence in our fair city and has already begun shipping crates of exotic finery and *objets d'art* to the site of her new mansion, all but completed as of this writing.

The Baroness, who came to international fame after parlaying her late husband's ailing estate into a veritable kingdom of wealth and political power, has spent the last eighteen months touring the world. She is accompanied in her travels by a small entourage of servants uncommon, few of whom are versed in the King's language and thus are best approached with patience and caution.

WAINSCOTTS TO INTRODUCE

Lord and Lady Wainscott have announced a grand ball to be held at their manor at week's end, at which time Baroness Cross will be formally introduced to Partington's favored citizens and its brokers of power.

BANKER MURDERED

EARS SLICED, STOLEN!

PARTINGTON police yesterday found the body of banker Charles X. Victor, a victim of foul play. While no suspects have yet been detained, Hughes' partner, Edgar Murchand, has himself posted a sizeable reward for any information leading to the arrest and prosecution of the villainous soul or souls responsible.

Most curious was the dissected state of Victor's corpse, leaving city wags to dub this the "Victorian Ear Mystery." No photoengravings have been released •••PLEASE CONTINUE INSIDE

....JUST ANOTHER DAY IN THE CITY OF PARTINGTON.

WELL, ONLY **ONE** OTHER, ACTUALLY.

THAT WOULD BE **SIMON**.

WHO'S DRAGGING ME OUT TO **WAINSCOTT MANOR** AND SOME **COMING OUT PARTY** FOR SOME OVER-SEAS ROYALTY OR SOME-SUCH FOL-DE-ROL... IN THE EVENT, I SUPPOSE, THAT MY **LINGUISTIC SKILLS** MIGHT BE OF SOME AID.

IT'S A QUARREL DIFFICULT TO **WIN** SEEING AS HOW, IN GENERAL, PEOPLE DON'T REALLY ENJOY **TALKING** TO HIM.

WHY... *ALL* OF THEM, I SUPPOSE...? WHY?

BECAUSE ONE WONDERS HOW MANY VALUABLES HE'S *ALREADY* FILCHED FROM THEIR *POCKETS* AND PASSED THROUGH THE WINDOW TO HIS ASSOCIATE *OUTSIDE.*

SHALL WE?

LET'S.

TRUTH TO TELL, IT DOESN'T MATTER *WHOSE* KITCHEN SIMON IS *IN.*

HE'LL *ALWAYS* STIR THE POT.

WHY, JUST TODAY, MY MEN HAD TO DEAL WITH AN ATTEMPTED RITUAL *SUICIDE* DOWNTOWN...A *MAD DOG* TERRORIZING THE DOCKS...*AND* A GANG OF TEENAGERS--

--TEENAGERS!--

--WHO WERE FENCING STOLEN GOODS TO FUEL THEIR *MEDICINAL CACOETHES!*

ADDICTIONS? TO WHAT?

THERE'S AN *OPIATE* PROBLEM DAWNING IN THIS TOWN. A WAVE OF *INEXPENSIVE DRUGS* IS SWEEPING PARTINGTON, TEMPTING THE YOUNG AND OLD ALIKE WITH AN UPLIFTING *EUPHORIA...*

...THAT, I PRESUME, TOO *OFTEN* ENDS IN *MADNESS.*

QUITE RIGHT. SIMON, YOU'VE BEEN COMPLAINING FOR *SOME TIME* THAT OUR FAIR BURG NO LONGER PRESENTS YOU WITH MEANINGFUL *CHALLENGES.*

I'D *GLADLY* SUFFER YOUR *ENNUI* AS THE PRICE *PAID* IF THAT WERE *TRUE,* BUT IT MAY *NOT* BE ERE *LONG.* ONE *CANNOT HELP* BUT *WONDER:*

WHATEVER NEW EVIL WILL VISIT US *NEXT?*

IF I MAY...

LADIES AND GENTLEMEN! AS PROUD *HOSTS* OF THE LATEST *VISITOR* TO PARTINGTON'S *SHORES*, LORD AND LADY WAINSCOTT ARE *HONORED* AT THIS TIME TO PRESENT, FRESH FROM *KHARIBAST*...

...THE BARONESS *MIRANDA CROSS* AND...

...oh, M–M–MY...

...A–AND HER MUH–MANSERVANT, A–*ANTAEUS.*

IS SHE COMING *THIS WAY?*

YOU'RE THE DETECTIVE.

YES, SIMON, YOU'VE *INTRIGUED* HER.

QUELLE SURPRISE.

WITH THE REWARD FROM THE **CARRINGTON AFFAIR**, SIMON REFURBISHED AN ABANDONED **CATHEDRAL** IN THE **NORTHSHIRE** PART OF TOWN AND MADE IT HIS **HOME** AND **HEADQUARTERS**. IT HOUSES SIMON'S **INVENTIONS**, HIS **LABORATORIES**, AND A LIBRARY **LEGENDARY** FOR ITS SIZE.

NEITHER **GATED** NOR **SECLUDED**, THE BUILDING IS **READILY ACCESSIBLE** TO **ALL**. NEVERTHELESS, WHILE OUR SERVICES SEEM OFTEN IN **DEMAND**, ONE DOESN'T SIMPLY WALK IN TO SIMON ARCHARD'S HOME AND ASK FOR **HELP**.

ADMITTANCE REQUIRES... QUITE **LITERALLY**...A "SCREENING PROCESS."

STATE YOUR BUSINESS.

NAME'S *MCCORKINDALE*. Y'WOU'NT *KNOW* ME...

...BUT A COME T'SEE MR. ARCHARD.

THE POOR MAN *TREMBLED*, THOUGH WHETHER A RESULT OF *NERVES* OR A *BOTTLE*, I COULD NOT SAY. NOT THAT YOU COULD *CONDEMN* HIM FOR SIPPING *WHISKEY*.

NOT WITH THE *SORROW* IN THOSE EYES.

...AWARE 'TAINT TH' KINDA HIGH-FALUTIN' CASE WHAT YOU'RE *KNOWN* F'R, SIR...

...BUT TH' BOYS DOWN A' THE *DOCK* PUT SOME COIN T'GETHER TO *HIRE* YE IF IT'S A QUESTION O' *MONEY*.

MONEY IS *NEVER* THE QUESTION. TELL ME ABOUT THE *VICTIM*.

O'SHAUGHNESSY IS--

--WAS-- HIS NAME. A *LEGENDARY* CAP'N IN HIS DAY HE WAS --B'LOVED BY *ALL* TH' DOCKWORKERS 'N' FISHERMEN, SIR. SWEARIN' NE'ER T'BREATHE NOTHIN' BUT *SALT AIR*, HE KEPT A RUM LI'L *SHACK* RIGHT THERE ON TH' *PIER*, AN' WE ALL *TENDED* T'HIM.

S'WHY WHA' *HAPPEN* MADE *NO* SENSE A'TALL.

RUN THROUGH A *DOZEN TIMES* 'RE MORE, HE WAS... KNIFED 'N' *GORED*...LEFT FLOATIN' UNDER THE *PIER*...BUT *WHY?* T'WEREN'T NO *ROBBERY*... O'SHAUGHNESSY NE'ER HAD TWO *PENNIES* T'JINGLE.

I IMAGINE *NOT*.

I CAN'T *HELP* YOU, McCORKINDALE. THIS IS A ROUTINE *POLICE* MATTER WIT NOT ENOUGH *CLUE*. AND TOO MANY *SUSPECTS*.

THE DOCKS ARE *FULL* OF UNSAVORY CHARACTERS AND GOINGS-ON. DOUBTLES THE OLD MAN SAW O OVERHEARD SOMETHIN THAT HE WASN'T *SUPPOSED* TO AND WAS *SILENCED*.

THAT'S THE ONLY *EXPLANATIO*

...

REALLY.

WHEN FORGER **EUGENE FEINSILBER** WAS KIDNAPPED FROM A **LOCKED PRISON CELL**, SIMON **YAWNED** AND SOLVED THE CASE WHILE COMPLETING A **CROSSWORD PUZZLE**.

WHEN THE DUCHESS OF LARTUUM'S ENTIRE **SUMMER HOME** WAS STOLEN RIGHT DOWN TO THE **STABLES**, HE PLACED A **TELEPHONE CALL** DURING HIS **MANICURE** AND MADE HEADLINES BEFORE **DINNER**.

THIS TIME, HE'S ACTUALLY ON HIS **FEET**. IS THERE SOMETHING TO THIS CASE THAT STRIKES A **CHORD** WITHIN HIM? DOES IT **MATTER**?

I DON'T THINK SO, SIR. SEE, THERE'S SOMETHIN' I HA'N'T MENTIONED YET. HE COULDN'TA HEARD **NOTHIN'** WHAT WOULD HAVE CAUSED ANYONE NO **TROUBLE**, 'CAUSIN' O'SHAUGHNESSY...

...HE WAS **BLIND 'N'** ALL BUT **DEAF**.

ALL I'M **SURE** OF IS THAT THERE'S A GLINT IN SIMON'S EYES I'VE NOT **SEEN** BEFORE.

AS THE AFTERNOON PROGRESSES, WE SORT THROUGH THE VICTIM O'SHAUGHNESSY'S PERSONAL EFFECTS... WE SPEAK TO THOSE WHO KNEW HIM...WE COMB HIS LAST-KNOWN WHEREABOUTS...ALL OF WHICH LEADS US TO...

BEFORE WE CAN MOVE A SINGLE STEP, THE FLAMES AND THE SMOKE ARE UPON US.

AND I KNOW IN THAT ONE MOMENT... THAT I HAVE LOST.

DESPITE SIMON'S IMPATIENT TOE-TAPPING, I REPAIR TO MY QUARTERS FOR A QUICK BATH AND CHANGE OF CLOTHING.

I SUPPOSE I COULD BE MOVING MORE QUICKLY, BUT I KNOW WHAT COMES NEXT.

VOTES FOR WOMEN

SHRIMP?

NICE. MOCK THE SHORT MAN.

WHO SAID I WAS REFERRING TO YOUR ENTIRE BODY?

DELIGHTFUL. STILL PUTTING THE "SUFFER" IN "SUFFRAGETTE," I SEE.

I CAN'T BELIEVE WE USED TO DATE.

SO I'M SEARCHING FOR ELEMENTS FOREI TO OUR SHORES.

SOMETHING I CAN TRACE TO A SPECIFIC REGION WOULD BE MOST HELPFUL.

AS DAEDALIAN AS SIMON CAN BE, EVEN A HEAD THAT INFLATED CAN HOLD ONLY SO MUCH INFORMATION.

WHICH IS WHY HE MAINTAINS A WORLDWIDE NETWORK OF AGENTS -- SPECIALISTS IN THEIR RESPECTIVE FIELDS. OTTO'S THE ONLY ONE I'VE EVER MET WHO'S LESS PERSONABLE THAN SIMON.

CERTAINLY. THERE MUST BE A TOY SHOPPE SOMEWHERE IN THE NEIGHBORHOOD.

AND I AM NOT SIMON'S SCRIVENER! I AM HIS PARTNER!

ASSISTANT.

READ THE NEWSPAPERS.

EXAMINE THE BUSINESS CARDS.

QUITE THE CHANGE FROM YOUR OLD PARTNER, SIMON. WHAT WAS HIS NAME AGAIN? LIGHT SOMETHING...

ON THE WALK BACK TO HEADQUARTERS, SIMON GROWS INCREASINGLY **REMOTE** AND **WITHDRAWN**.

I DON'T TAKE IT **PERSONALLY,** EVEN AFTER I'M FORCED TO GUIDE HIM BY THE **ELBOW.**

I DO, HOWEVER, WALK HIM THROUGH THE OCCASIONAL **PUDDLE** JUST FOR THE FUN OF IT.

UNDER THOSE RARE CIRCUMSTANCES WHERE SIMON IS **TRULY** PERPLEXED, HE HONES HIS CONCENTRATION BY CLAMBERING INSIDE A BEASTLY CONTRAPTION OF HIS OWN DESIGN--

--A SORT OF **REVERSE BATHYSPHERE** DESIGNED TO DEPRIVE HIM OF EXTRANEOUS **SENSORY INPUT.**

HE CALLS IT HIS "**THINK TANK.**" WHILE I CANCEL HIS **APPOINTMENTS** FOR THE DAY...

...HE PREPARES FOR **IMMERSION.**

WITH MY AFTERNOON SUDDENLY **FREE,** I ELECT TO DO SOME INVESTIGATING OF MY **OWN.**

THE LAST TIME WE SAW THEOPOLOUS AS WE **RECOGNIZE** HIM WAS AT THE PARTY HOSTED BY...

...LADY **WAINSCOTT.** FORGIVE ME FOR STOPPING BY **UNANNOUNCED,** BUT I NEED TO ASK YOU SOME **QUESTIONS...**

AND YOU **ARE...?**

...ON BEHALF OF **SIMON ARCHARD.**

OH! OH, OF **COURSE! ELLA,** ISN'T IT?

EMMA.

YOU'RE SIMON'S LITTLE **HELPER,** AREN'T YOU? WHAT CAN I **DO** FOR YOU, ELLA?

⇒**SIGH**⇐

IT'S ABOUT **COMMISSIONER THORNTON,** YOUR LADYSHIP. DID HIS DEMEANOR THE OTHER NIGHT SEEM **NORMAL** TO YOU...?

WHY, I...I **SUPPOSE...**

AGATHA, WHO'S AT THE **DOOR?**

AGATHA!

LORD **WAINSCOTT,** SIR, IF I MAY HAVE A **MOMENT**--

YOU MOST CERTAINLY MAY **NOT.**

AUBREGINE, DEAR, IS SOMETHING THE **MATTER?**

NOTHING THAT CAN'T BE CARRIED AWAY IN THE **FASTEST TAXICAB,** AGATHA. NO ONE IN **THIS** HOUSE WILL BE INCONVENIENCED FOR **ONE MOMENT** BY ANY AGENT OF **SIMON ARCHARD'S!**

YOU CAN REMIND YOUR **EMPLOYER,** MISS BISHOP--

⇒**SNFFF**⇐

--THAT THE **WAINSCOTT FORTUNE** CARRIES WITH IT GREAT **INFLUENCE** IN THIS CITY--

--AND THE **TOWN FATHERS** HAVE HAD **QUITE ENOUGH** OF SIMON ARCHARD'S PECULIAR BRAND OF **CELEBRITY!**

HE THINKS THE **REST** OF US ARE AT HIS **BECK** AND **CALL?** TELL HIM I'LL HAVE A DAMN **HIGHWAY** PUT THROUGH HIS **HOME** IF HE DOESN'T START REMEMBERING HIS **PLACE!**

GOOD **DAY,** MADAM!

NO.

NO, NOT AT **ALL.**

AND SO THE **AFTERNOON**. WHEREVER I **GO**, A GRUFF **RECEPTION**.

IT'S AS IF ALL THE MEN OF **POWER** IN PARTINGTON ABANDONED THEIR REGARD FOR SIMON AND HIS DOINGS **OVERNIGHT**.

OR, RATHER, I SHOULD SAY OVER NIGHTS...**TWO**...COINCIDING WITH THE ARRIVAL OF **BARONESS MIRANDA CROSS** TO OUR CITY...

...AND NO DETECTIVE WORTH A FIG TAKES **COINCIDENCE** SERIOUSLY.

...AND HOW WAS SHE ABLE TO **RESIST** MY **CONTROL**?

...IS...MY GOD...

A DISCREET **CARRIAGE RIDE** BRINGS ME TO HER ESTATE-IN-**PROCESS** -- AN ABANDONED CASTLE WHICH CREWS HAVE BEGUN **REFURBISHING** TO HER QUESTIONABLE TASTE.

WHAT DID I **EXPECT** BY **COMING** HERE? THAT SHE WOULD INVITE ME IN FOR **TEA** SO THAT SHE MIGHT **EXPLAIN** HERSELF...

E SEEMS TO HAVE POWERS TO MATCH **OWN**...TO **EXCEED** THEM...BUT **THAT** IS FORMATION I HAVE NO CHOICE BUT TO EP **PRIVATE**.

I CANNOT CONFER WITH SIMON ABOUT WHAT I SAW DURING THE **FIRE** WITHOUT REVEALING MY **OWN** SECRETS -- AND I **CANNOT** YET TELL SIMON ABOUT MY ABILITIES. I **CAN NOT**. THE **CONSEQUENCES**...

EFORE LAST NIGHT, HE PRICE FOR THEIR SE WAS **FORFEITURE** OF ALL I **KNOW**. NOW, PPARENTLY, THE COST S THAT THE BARONESS VILL TAKE THEM FOR ER **OWN**...OR SO SHE AYS...AND, PRESUMABLY, SE THEM **AGAINST** US.

SHE MAY BE **LYING**. BUT FOR **SIMON'S** SAKE, I CANNOT TAKE THAT **RISK**.

WHY WOULD SHE WISH US **HARM**? DID HER PRESENCE ON THE **FISHING BOAT** PROVE A CONNECTION TO ILLICIT **ACTIVITIES**?

AND HOW IS SHE BEHIND THE SUDDEN **SEA CHANGE** IN SIMON'S **POPULARITY**? HOW COULD **ANY** MAN BE INFLUENCED BY A WOMAN WITH SUCH OBVIOUSLY GAUDY AND ECCENTRIC **TASTES**?

WHY, THAT GHASTLY WINDOW **ALONE** IS...

...IS EVIDENCE.

I HAVE TO GO. I HAVE TO REPORT THIS TO **SIMON**...

...BEFORE I AM **SEEN**.

"I **TOLD** YOU, ANTAEUS..."

AS PROMISED, MY RETURN TRIP TAKES ME PAST OTTO'S **LAB** TO RETRIEVE HIS **REPORT**.

Oh...!

THERE WON'T BE ONE.

THE BARONESS. I DON'T KNOW WHY, OR HOW...

...BUT SHE'S **BEHIND** THIS. I **KNOW** IT.

A DAY LATER, I DON'T KNOW WHETHER TO BE WORRIED FOR OR ANGRY AT SIMON.

WHILE HARDLY A PARAGON OF *WARMTH*, HE'D STILL WANT TO BE *PRESENT* AS WE BURY ONE OF HIS *ASSOCIATES*. THIS, I *KNOW*.

TOO *WELL*.

HAS THE BARONESS ALSO GOTTEN TO *SIMON* SOMEHOW, WITHOUT DISCLOSING HER TRIUMPH TO *ME*?

I DOUBT IT. JUDGING BY HER BEHAVIOR AT THE *FIRE*, SHE'D WANT *ME* TO *KNOW*.

NO *AUTOPSY* WAS NECESSARY. THE AUTHORITIES, FRANKLY, COULDN'T *WAIT* TO GET OTTO INTO THE *GROUND*. BLESS HIS SOUL, HE COUNTED AMONG HIS COMPATRIOTS ONLY A HANDFUL OF SIMON'S FELLOW *OPERATIVES*. BARTLESBY THE MOUCH... THE ABBESS *LADYBIRD NELL*... A FEW OTHERS...

...HARDLY A FITTING *FUNEREAL PARTY* FOR EVEN A MAN OF OTTO'S SOUR DISPOSITION. IF HE HAD ANY *FAMILY*...

--GATHERED HERE PAY *FINAL RESPECTS* THE DECEASED--

HAD T'GO HEARIN' ABOUT THIS IN THE *PENNYSHEETS*, Y'BLOODY *SHORTWANK*...

...LEF ME QUITE ITCH T'SC WI' YE, BR OTTO.

THE *DEAD?* THERE AIN'T NO WORDS *FOUL* ENOUGH. YE THINK YERSELVES HIS *FRIENDS?* NO.

WHILE THE ABBESS AND THE PRIEST RELIEVE THEMSELVES OF THE CONTENTS OF THEIR **STOMACHS**, WE TRY OUR **BEST** TO SALVAGE OTTO'S **DIGNITY**...

...BUT THERE ARE TOO **MANY** OF THE WRIGGLING LARVAE... AND THEY'LL FIND OTTO SOONER THAN LATER, **ANYWAY**. WITH GRIEF MORE PROFOUND THAN **BEFORE**, WE EASE OTTO INTO THE **EARTH**... AND SING A **PRAYER** THOUGH WE'RE ONE VOICE **SHORT**.

SIMON...

...WHERE ARE YOU

CONTINUED & NEXT ISSUE

CHAPTER 3

I COULD HAVE TAKEN A CARRIAGE BACK FROM OTTO'S FUNERAL.

I ELECT TO WALK.

*IT'LL DULL THE IMPULSE TO BURY SIMON RIGHT **NEXT** TO HIM.*

EVEN THOUGH SIMON ARCHARD HURTLES THROUGH LIFE WITH THE COMPASSION OF A **THROWN BRICK**, IT'S **UNFORGIVABLE** THAT HE WOULD **IGNORE** A MEMORIAL SERVICE FOR ONE OF HIS **OWN OPERATIVES**.

IT'S NOT AS IF SIMON'S MET WITH FOUL PLAY **HIMSELF**. IF **THAT** WERE THE CASE, I WOULD HAVE... BEEN **NOTIFIED**.

BUT EVEN IF HE'S DOGMATICALLY FOLLOWING A NEW LEAD ON THE **OPIATE SMUGGLING** CASE, NOTHING--AND I MEAN **NOTHING**-- KEEPS SIMON FROM **DEVOURING** THE WARES OF THE **CORNER NEWS VENDORS**.

SIMON **PRIDES** HIMSELF ON STAYING INFORMED ON ALL MATTERS REGARDING THE CITY OF PARTINGTON--AND OTTO'S **DEATH** HEADLINED **EVERY BROADSHEET**.

WHICH BRINGS US BACK TO *"UNFORGIVABLE."*

HOWEVER, ONCE I LAY EYES ON **47 STRAND** ONCE MORE...

...SUDDENLY, BEATING AN **EXCUSE** OUT OF SIMON IS THE **LAST** THING ON MY MIND.

AS IT HAPPENS, WHILE I'VE BEEN BUSY CONDEMNING **SIMON**...

...SOMEONE **ELSE** HAS BEEN CONDEMNING HIS **HEADQUARTERS**.

WHAT THE **DEVIL**...?

OFFICER, WHAT'S THE **MEANING** OF THIS?

MISS **BISHOP**, IS IT? MISS BISHOP, WE'LL HAVE **NAE TROUBLE** HERE FROM THE LIKES O' **YOU**.

"THE **LIKES** OF..."?

WAIT. OVER **THERE**. THE MEN GIVING THE **ORDERS** --

-- THEY'RE THE **MAYOR** OF PARTINGTON -- **AND** THE **BANKER**, WHO --

--DECONSECRATED OR **NOT**, **NEVER** SHOULD HAVE SOLD SUCH A **SACRED BUILDING** TO SUCH A **PROFANE MARPLOT!** MY MOST SINCERE **APOLOGIES**, MAYOR!

I **AGREE** IT'S A **SIN** TO SEE THIS CATHEDRAL GO FROM **NO** USE TO **ILL** USE, PERTHANBY --

-- AND I'M **INCLINED** SIMPLY TO BURN IT TO THE **GROUND** TO ALLEVIATE THE STINK OF **HERESY** FROM ITS RAFTERS!

YOU **HEARD** ME, MISS BISHOP!

BOTH OF THESE MEN HAVE ALWAYS BEEN STAUNCH **SUPPORTERS** OF SIMON'S **ACTIVITIES**. THEIR SUDDEN **TURNABOUT PERPLEXES** ME...

...UNTIL I SEE THEM DIP **SNUFF** FROM BOXES OF A CHILLINGLY FAMILIAR **DESIGN**...

NOT ALL OF SIMON'S OPERATIVES ARE ON A **PAYROLL**. MANY OF TH- LESS FREQUENTLY **CONSULTED**-- PARTICULARLY THOSE WHO ARE WELL- TO-DO **THEMSELVES**--LEND THEIR SERVICES IN EXCHANGE FOR PAST **FAVOR**

HEADMASTER **WARREN SUMMERSBY** (**PARTINGTON UNIVERSITY**, FOR EXAM

AT SIMON'S BEHEST, SUMMERSBY KEEP. WATCH OVER HIS BEST AND BRIGHTES STUDENTS WITH AN EYE TOWARDS WHICH ONES MAY, IN TIME, BECOME EITHER **ALLIES** OR **ADVERSARIES**.

THE DAMAGE TO OTTO'S **BODY** WAS **INCONSISTENT** WITH THE SIZE OF THE SHELF THAT "FELL" ON HIM. SINCE THERE WAS NO **AUTOPSY** AND OTTO WAS, FOLLOWING HIS PROCLAIMED WISHES, BURIED **SANS ENBALMING**...

...THE MAGGOTS WERE MY WAY OF LEECHING ENOUGH FLUID FROM OTTO'S **SYSTEM** TO DETERMINE IF HE WAS **POISONED** RATHER THAN **CRUSHED**.

AND HE **WAS**.

MOREOVER, THE LARVAE AND THIS **SMUGGLED PHIAL** TEST CONSISTENTLY WITH EACH **OTHER**. THIS INDICATES THAT OTTO WAS INJECTED WITH A FATAL DOSE OF THE VERY OPIATE THE BARONESS IS USING TO MANIPULATE HER **VICTIMS**.

ASTOUNDING. OTTO **CONTINUES** TO AID US FROM BEYON THE **GRAVE**. HE--

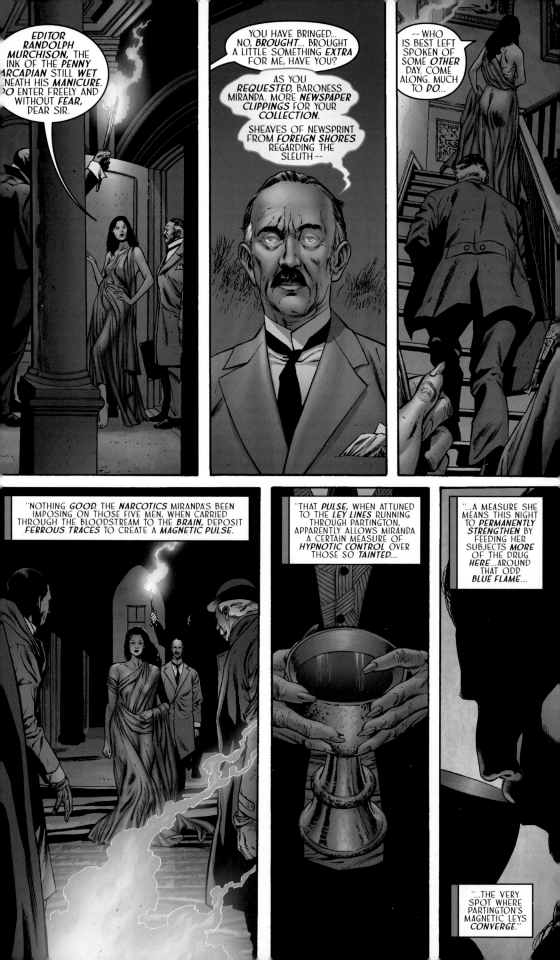

EDITOR RANDOLPH MURCHISON, THE INK OF THE PENNY ARCADIAN STILL WET NEATH HIS MANICURE. DO ENTER FREELY AND WITHOUT FEAR, DEAR SIR.

YOU HAVE BRINGED... NO, BROUGHT... BROUGHT A LITTLE SOMETHING EXTRA FOR ME, HAVE YOU?

AS YOU REQUESTED, BARONESS MIRANDA. MORE NEWSPAPER CLIPPINGS FOR YOUR COLLECTION.

SHEAVES OF NEWSPRINT FROM FOREIGN SHORES REGARDING THE SLEUTH --

-- WHO IS BEST LEFT SPOKEN OF SOME OTHER DAY. COME ALONG. MUCH TO DO...

"NOTHING GOOD. THE NARCOTICS MIRANDA'S BEEN IMPOSING ON THOSE FIVE MEN, WHEN CARRIED THROUGH THE BLOODSTREAM TO THE BRAIN, DEPOSIT FERROUS TRACES TO CREATE A MAGNETIC PULSE.

"THAT PULSE, WHEN ATTUNED TO THE LEY LINES RUNNING THROUGH PARTINGTON, APPARENTLY ALLOWS MIRANDA A CERTAIN MEASURE OF HYPNOTIC CONTROL OVER THOSE SO TAINTED...

"...A MEASURE SHE MEANS THIS NIGHT TO PERMANENTLY STRENGTHEN BY FEEDING HER SUBJECTS MORE OF THE DRUG HERE...AROUND THAT ODD BLUE FLAME...

"...THE VERY SPOT WHERE PARTINGTON'S MAGNETIC LEYS CONVERGE."

BEFORE THE BARONESS ARRIVED, SIMON AND I ENJOYED **NUMEROUS** ADVENTURES FRAUGHT WITH PERIL, TINGED WITH DANGER.

THEY WERE **EASY** TO ENJOY BECAUSE NO ONE WAS AT **RISK**, NOT **REALLY**.

BEFORE THE BARONESS ARRIVED.

NOW WE'RE GOING TO **DIE**.

I CAN'T EVEN USE ANY OF THE **PROTECTIVE MAGIC** I'VE KEPT SECRET FROM SIMON BECAUSE THE SECOND I DO...

...I'LL TAKE IT **FROM** YOU JUST LIKE **THAT** AND TURN IT **AGAINST** YOU IN WAYS **BEYOND** YOUR FEEBLE **IMAGININGS**. BUT **DO** TRY. DO **SOMETHING** TO CHALLENGE ME. THIS...

"...THIS IS SIMPLY **TOO** EASY."

EMMA, THE **FIRE**!

THE FIRE!

THIS IS NOT AT ALL THE WAY IT SUPPOSED TO **END** FOR US.

BIGGER? DESPAIR HITS ME LIKE A *FIST.* THE REQUEST MAKES NO SENSE AT ALL. HAS SIMON *HIMSELF* SUCCUMBED TO MIRANDA'S NIGHTMARISH BIDDING?

OR SHOULD I SURRENDER MY *FAITH* TO HIS PREPOSTEROUS *COMMAND?*

HEAVEN HELP ME, EVEN IF I *COULD* ACT...

AAAAH!

YOU *WITCH!* YOU'LL *NEVER*--

...GIVEN THE *MADNESS* AND *CONFUSION* SWIRLING *ABOUT* ME...

Oh, *PLEASE.* DO YOU *TRULY* WISH YOUR *FINAL WORDS* TO BE THAT MUCH OF A *CLICHÉ?* EMMA... I'LL *ALWAYS.*

...SIMON...

ALL THAT YOU *KNOW,* ALL YOU CAN *CONCEIVE*...I AND OTHERS *LIKE* ME ARE *FATED* TO *CONTROL* IT.

...SIMON, *FORGIVE* ME...

SO IS IT *WRITTEN,* SO SHALL IT *BE.* I MYSELF HAVE STUDIED *BODEMENTS.* MAPS OF *DESTINY.*

...BUT I DON'T *KNOW* IF I COULD--

PROPHECIES.

--TRUST *YOU.*

SWELL THE *BLAZE.* HOW?

SMAK

AAAH!

IF HE THINKS THIS IS AN APPROPRIATE TIME FOR HIM TO TAKE A **SOLO WALKABOUT,** HE'S **MISTAKEN.**

THIS TIME, I'M GOING TO **FIND** HIM NO MATTER THAT I HAVE TO PUT ALL OUR **RESOURCES** TO THE **TASK.**

I'M GOING TO FIND HIM AND **CONFRONT** HIM ABOUT THIS.

I'VE GOTTEN THE STRANGE FEELING AS THIS CASE HAS PROGRESSED THAT SIMON DOESN'T **TRUST** ME AS HE USED TO...BUT I CAN'T IMAGINE **WHY.**

WHATEVER THE **REASON** MIGHT BE...

...LET'S HO IT'S NOT PERMANEN

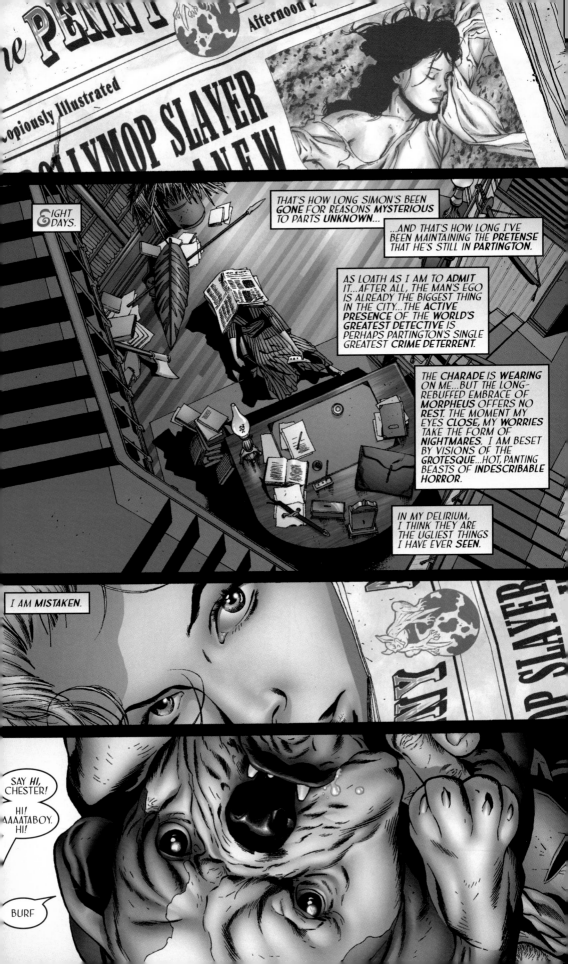

The PENNY

Afternoon 2

Copiously Illustrated

OLLYMOP SLAYER
ANEW

EIGHT DAYS.

THAT'S HOW LONG SIMON'S BEEN *GONE* FOR REASONS *MYSTERIOUS* TO PARTS *UNKNOWN*...

...AND THAT'S HOW LONG I'VE BEEN MAINTAINING THE *PRETENSE* THAT HE'S STILL IN *PARTINGTON*.

AS LOATH AS I AM TO *ADMIT* IT...AFTER ALL, THE MAN'S EGO IS ALREADY THE BIGGEST THING IN THE CITY...THE *ACTIVE PRESENCE* OF THE *WORLD'S GREATEST DETECTIVE* IS PERHAPS PARTINGTON'S SINGLE GREATEST *CRIME DETERRENT*.

THE *CHARADE* IS WEARING ON ME...BUT THE LONG-REBUFFED EMBRACE OF *MORPHEUS* OFFERS NO REST. THE MOMENT MY EYES *CLOSE*, MY *WORRIES* TAKE THE FORM OF *NIGHTMARES*. I AM BESET BY VISIONS OF THE *GROTESQUE*...HOT, PANTING BEASTS OF *INDESCRIBABLE* HORROR.

IN MY DELIRIUM, I THINK THEY ARE THE UGLIEST THINGS I HAVE EVER *SEEN*.

I AM *MISTAKEN*.

SAY *HI*, CHESTER!

HI! AAAATABOY. HI!

BURF

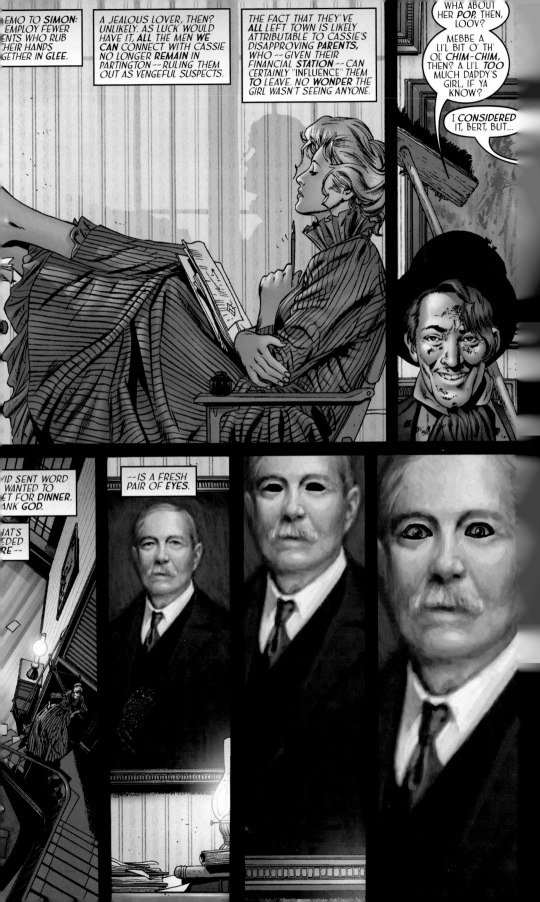

NOTHING.

TEN O'CLOCK. ELEVEN. TWELVE. ONE.

FOUR HOURS, AND NOT ONE NIBBLE.

A TERM I USE STRICTLY IN THE *FISHING* SENSE, BY THE WAY. NOT THAT I'M PARTICULARLY *EAGER* TO BE TAKEN SERIOUSLY AS SOME *TOFFER*...

...BUT... I MEAN... IS IT *ME*?

AM I DOING SOMETHING *WRONG*, OR--

OH.

COVER 6

Jeff **JOHNSON** · PENCILER
Mark **PENNINGTON** · INKER
Laura **DePUY** · COLORIST

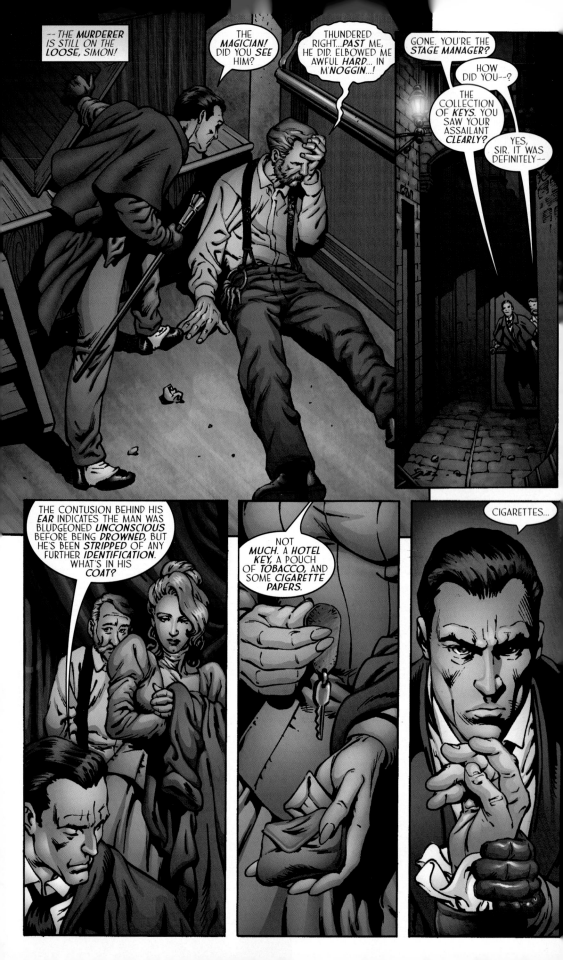

SIMON, HOW DID YOU KNOW..? THE *FIRST* VICTIM'S FINGERS SHOWED NO *NICOTINE STAINS*... YET HE'D PURCHASED TOBACCO AND CIGARETTE PAPERS FOR *SOMEONE*, PRESUMABLY A *TRAVELING COMPANION*...AND THE *BEETON* OPERATIVES TRAVEL IN *PAIRS*.

GIVEN THAT FAR MORE *MEN* THAN *WOMEN* ENGAGE IN THE NASTY HABIT OF ROLLING *CIGARETTES*, ODDS WERE THAT COMPANION WAS HIS *INVESTIGATIVE PARTNER* -- AND THUS ANOTHER *TARGET*.

SINCE CORRADINO COULDN'T COMMIT *BOTH* MURDERS ON *STAGE*, HE ARRANGED FOR THE *POISON*...NO DOUBT ONE OF *MANY* CONTINGENCIES...

...THEN STOLE THE FIRST VICTIM'S *IDENTIFICATION* HOPING TO *STALL* ME...

...GIVING THIS MAN TIME TO *DIE*.

William Corradine a.k.a. "The Astounding Corradino"

Link suspected between suspect's *touring dates* and mysterious robberies committed *dates* same. Keep Cor...

BUT HOW COULD CORRADINO *POSSIBLY* SURMISE ONLY *ONE* OF THEM WOULD COME TO HIS *SHOW?*

SIMON, WE *ALSO* RECEIVED V.I.P. TICKETS. WHAT *CONCEIVABLE REASON* WOULD CORRADINO HAVE TO INVITE THE WORLD'S *FOREMOST DETECTIVE* TO THE *SCENE* OF HIS *CRIME?*

TO *TAUNT* ME. ALL OF THIS *CONFIRMS* WHAT I'D ALREADY *SUSPECTED*... I AND, APPARENTLY, *MIRANDA CROSS*, WHO GATHERED *NEWSPAPER CLIPPINGS* ON OUR MAGICIAN.

"CORRADINO" IS BUT AN *ALIAS* THE MAN MAINTAINS.

HIS TRUE NAME IS *LIGHTBOURNE*.

IT'S OVER *HERE.*

HIM? LAST I SAW OF *HIM,* HE WAS *OVERWROUGHT* ABOUT THE *MURDER.*

THE POOR MAN SIMPLY WENT TO *PIECES.*

...AND WHILE I *FREED* YOU, LIGHTBOURNE *ESCAPED*.

SIMON, THOSE *CLIPPINGS* YOU WERE SO DESPERATE TO SALVAGE FROM MIRANDA CROSS' MANSION... DID THEY HAVE ANYTHING TO DO WITH...

...MY *EX-PARTNER?* PERHAPS. WE CAN DISCUSS THAT LATER. YOU SAY YOU LIBERATED A *BANDANA...?*

YOU MEAN *THIS?* I SUPPOSE I GRABBED IT *FROM* HIM WITHOUT TRULY *THINKING* ABOUT IT. IS IT *SIGNIFICANT?*

YES.

AND YOU'LL TELL ME WHY WHEN YOU *FEEL* LIKE IT?

YES.

WELL, *SPLEND* THAT'S THE SIMON I *KNOW*...

...*NOT* THE SIMON WHO SO UNCHARACTERISTICALLY *EXPLODED* MOMENTS AGO. I'VE *NEVER* SEEN HIM LIKE *THAT. EVER.*

WHAT IS IT ABOUT THIS OLD ALLY OF SIMON'S THAT CAN BRING *OUT* SUCH BEHAVIOR?

WHAT *IS* THE MYSTERY OF *LIGHTBOURNE?*

4262005

3 1191 00744 1108